Possible RULES FOR contest

nuggets by Celes...

Who can eat the most nuggets?

Frank — too easy

20 nuggets a day
20×30 = 600 nuggets

keep it simple

100 nuggets a day
100×30 days = 3000 nuggets

1000 nuggets a day
1000×30 days = 30,000 nuggets
total — too easy

Each day, nuggets double

Day	nuggets
1	1
2	2
3	4
4	8
5	16
6	32
7	64
8	128
9	256 ...

~~double the nuggets the last person ate~~
~~double the nuggets you ate yesterday~~
~~two more nuggets than~~ Double nugget amount, everyday for ~~100 days~~ ~~30 days~~ ~~10 days~~ — not enough nuggets. Or time.

projected moment of monster nugget saturation (MMNS)

MMNS

50 Days?

536,870,912 — 8000+ tons
(15 × 536,870,912 = 8,053,063,680 grams of nuggets

Daily nugget production 8000 tons in a day?

BOOKS TO CHECK

• Monsters: a guide
• SO, YOU'VE BEEN STALKED BY A MONSTER
• MY JOURNEY INTO MONSTER COUNTRY, AND MY TERRIBLE MISTAKE WITH CHICKEN NUGGETS
• Exponential growth

Moat... pheric bubbles?

The Legend of Sissa ibn Dahir

According to legend, Sissa ibn Dahir was a wise man who lived in India around fifteen hundred years ago. There are many stories of Sissa, but perhaps the most famous is a story that some believe shows the origins of the game Chaturanga, considered to be the ancestor to modern chess.

In the legend, a king asks for a game to be invented that would entertain him. Sissa invented a game on a sixty-four square board using pieces that moved in ... ways ... choosing. ... the king was delighted. So happy was he that he offered Sissa ... humble man," said Sissa. 'All I would ask is just one ... more fitting reward for such a ... its own greatness

"Very well," said Sissa. "Shou... to reward me, I would ask for ... wheat today. The next day, I s... two. Then four the following ... and so on until the wheat ha... thirty days. At that time, yo... true value of the gift that y... me."

They call this man wise, t... does not know the value of h... low price makes for a high y...

"Sissa, it shall be as yo... But I warn you, this c... us is binding, and no... in any way. You shal... as I have received y... will set forth happy...

"Your majesty, i... presence there is ... ... I gladly...

For Emily and Fionn
and the joy that you bring.
–T.B.

Balzer + Bray is an imprint of HarperCollins Publishers.

One Chicken Nugget
Copyright © 2023 by Tadgh Bentley
All rights reserved. Manufactured in Italy.
No part of this book may be used or reproduced in any manner whatsoever without written permission
except in the case of brief quotations embodied in critical articles and reviews. For information address
HarperCollins Children's Books, a division of HarperCollins Publishers, 195 Broadway, New York, NY 10007.
www.harpercollinschildrens.com

Library of Congress Control Number: 2022933248
ISBN 978-0-06-268982-5

The artist used Procreate to create the digital illustrations for this book.
Typography by Caitlin Stamper
Hand lettering by Julia Christians
22 23 24 25 26 RTLO 10 9 8 7 6 5 4 3 2 1
❖
First Edition

ONE CHICKEN NUGGET

by TADGH BENTLEY

BALZER + BRAY
An Imprint of HarperCollins*Publishers*

Everybody knows monsters love chicken nuggets,
but Frank loved them more than most.
Think about how much you love your favorite food and double it.
Then double it again.
That's how much Frank loved his nuggets.

Well, really he loved *Celeste's* nuggets.
Frank could smell those golden wonders
from miles away.

Celeste's chicken nuggets had the perfect balance of tender juiciness and crispy crunch.

Her dipping sauces were sensational.

And her seasonings? Celestial.
Frank couldn't get enough.

But Celeste had had enough of Frank.
He was not exactly an ideal customer.

He behaved, frankly, like a monster.
And monsters are not good for business.

Celeste tried everything she could think of to get rid of him . . .
But nothing worked.

Finally, after he had cleaned her out yet again, Celeste threw up her hands.
"Just how many chicken nuggets can you eat?"

"A million!" Frank laughed. "No, double a million! Double *that*!"
Celeste slumped. She was out of ideas. And out of chicken nuggets.

So she closed up shop and drove to the library.
She consulted cookbooks and business books.
She studied up on marketing and math.
She read folklore and literature.
And soon she'd cooked up a new idea.

The next morning Celeste announced a monthlong contest of monstrous proportions.

She explained the rules to the gathering crowd: "The first day, everyone gets one chicken nugget. Each day after that, you have to eat twice as many nuggets as the day before—"
"Easy peasy!" crowed Frank.
"If you can do this for *thirty* days, you'll win free chicken nuggets for life!"

30 DAY DOUBLE NUGGET CHALLENGE
DOUBLE OR NOTHING
NUGGET EATING CHALLENGE
How many nuggets can you eat in 30 days?
Every day, the number of nuggets will DOUBLE
Day 1
Day 2
Day 3
Day 4
Day 5
Day 6
WINNER WINNER CHICKEN DINNER
FREE NUGGETS FOREVER*
*or leave and never return

And so the contest began
with a single nugget.
Frank dipped his in barbecue sauce,
savoring its juicy goodness.

Then he licked each finger, winked at Celeste,
and sauntered off.

The next day, the number doubled to two nuggets.

The third day meant four nuggets.

Day 2
2
nuggets

Day 3
4
nuggets

Day 4
8
nuggets

Some little kids dropped out of the contest after day five.
But not Frank. This was barely a morsel for a monster like him.

Day 5
16

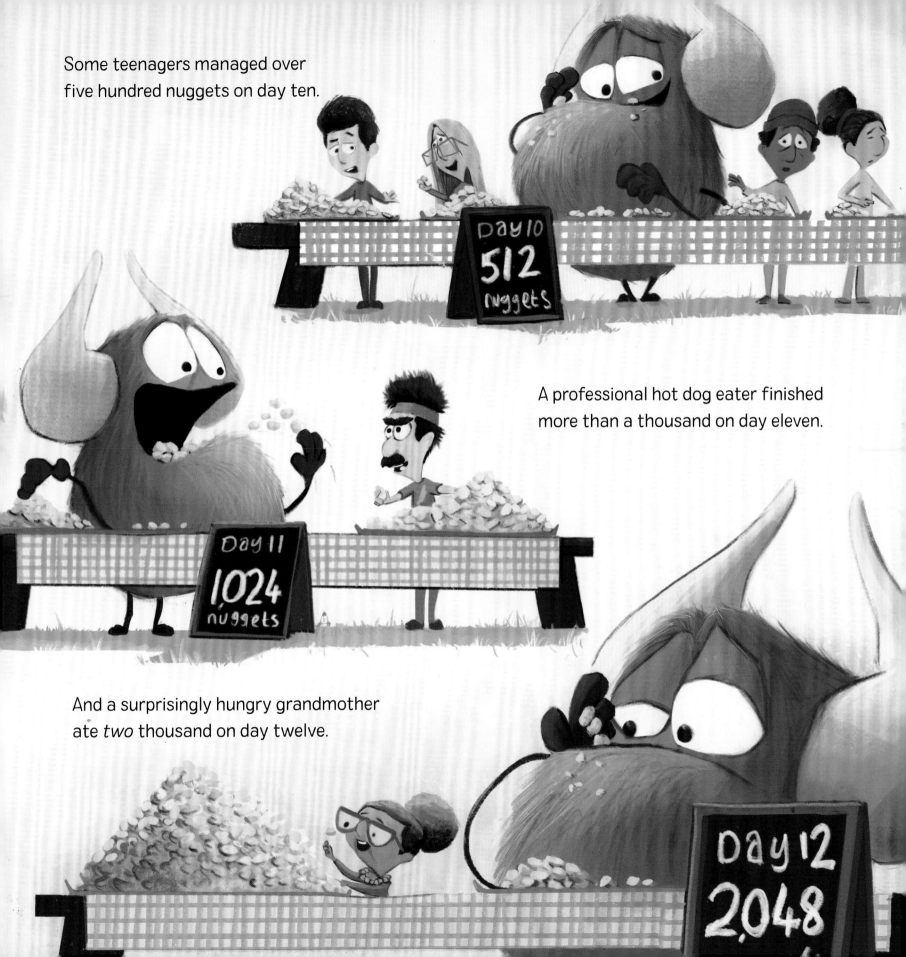

Some teenagers managed over five hundred nuggets on day ten.

Day 10
512 nuggets

A professional hot dog eater finished more than a thousand on day eleven.

Day 11
1,024 nuggets

And a surprisingly hungry grandmother ate *two* thousand on day twelve.

Day 12
2,048

But by day fourteen, Frank was the only contestant left.
He licked his fingers, winked at Celeste, and swaggered off.

Each day, the crowd grew. Just how many chicken nuggets
could one monster eat? How many could Celeste *make*?
A cheer went up when Frank ate his one millionth nugget
on day twenty-one.
Now, that is a lot of nuggets—

for anyone but a monster like Frank.

The very next day, Frank ate *two* million nuggets.

And the day after that he ate *four* million.

By day twenty-five, Celeste's fryer was creaking
and her batter reserves were running low.

DAY 25
16,777,216
nuggets

Would she be feeding this monster for life?

But all the doubling was beginning
to be troubling for Frank.

After swallowing over thirty-three million
nuggets on day twenty-six,

He licked his fingers, winked at Celeste,
and *tried* to swagger off . . .

But frankly, it was more of a stagger.

And on day twenty-nine, Frank finally had to admit . . .
he was starting to feel a wee bit full.

But he still ate every nugget, all two hundred million
of them—with barbecue sauce.

Finally, it was day thirty. Five hundred and thirty-six million, eight hundred and seventy thousand, nine hundred and twelve chicken nuggets.

Which is a lot. Even for a monster like Frank.

Celeste cooked and Frank ate. And cooked. And ate.
And cooked and ate some more.
The crowd was transfixed. (And a bit frightened.)

nuggets
by Celeste

After three hundred million nuggets,
Frank felt a little movement in his tummy.
After four hundred million, he felt a rumbling.
After *five* hundred million nuggets,
Frank's tummy was tumbling.

But, finally, he was just one nugget away from a *lifetime* of nuggets.
Nothing but delicious chicken nuggets, forever and ever.

He lifted the last crispy morsel to his bread crumb–covered face . . .
and then . . . it happened . . .

Frank felt quite a bit better after that.
(The crowd felt quite a bit worse.)
And Celeste felt utterly stunned

as the monster dipped the final chicken nugget in barbecue sauce,

gave one last heavy-lidded wink, and . . .

. . . handed it to her.

Even for a monster like Frank,
more than a trillion chicken nuggets
was quite enough for a lifetime.
He never wanted to see another nugget
ever again.

Though hot dogs were a different story . . .

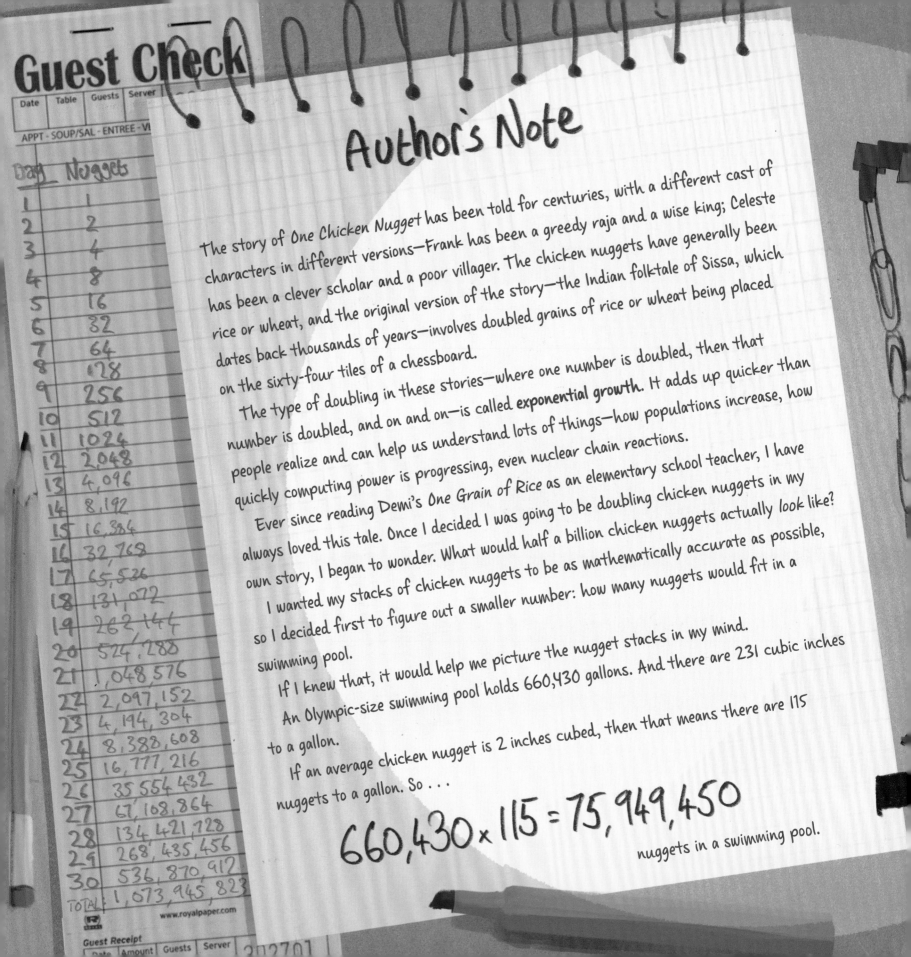

Guest Check

Date	Table	Guests	Server

APPT - SOUP/SAL - ENTREE - VE

Day	Nuggets
1	1
2	2
3	4
4	8
5	16
6	32
7	64
8	128
9	256
10	512
11	1,024
12	2,048
13	4,096
14	8,192
15	16,384
16	32,768
17	65,536
18	131,072
19	262,144
20	524,288
21	1,048,576
22	2,097,152
23	4,194,304
24	8,388,608
25	16,777,216
26	35,554,432
27	67,108,864
28	134,421,728
29	268,435,456
30	536,870,912
TOTAL	1,073,945,823

www.royalpaper.com

Guest Receipt
Date | Amount | Guests | Server

Author's Note

The story of One Chicken Nugget has been told for centuries, with a different cast of characters in different versions—Frank has been a greedy raja and a wise king; Celeste has been a clever scholar and a poor villager. The chicken nuggets have generally been rice or wheat, and the original version of the story—the Indian folktale of Sissa, which dates back thousands of years—involves doubled grains of rice or wheat being placed on the sixty-four tiles of a chessboard.

The type of doubling in these stories—where one number is doubled, then that number is doubled, and on and on—is called **exponential growth**. It adds up quicker than people realize and can help us understand lots of things—how populations increase, how quickly computing power is progressing, even nuclear chain reactions.

Ever since reading Demi's One Grain of Rice as an elementary school teacher, I have always loved this tale. Once I decided I was going to be doubling chicken nuggets in my own story, I began to wonder. What would half a billion chicken nuggets actually look like? I wanted my stacks of chicken nuggets to be as mathematically accurate as possible, so I decided first to figure out a smaller number: how many nuggets would fit in a swimming pool.

If I knew that, it would help me picture the nugget stacks in my mind.

An Olympic-size swimming pool holds 660,430 gallons. And there are 231 cubic inches to a gallon.

If an average chicken nugget is 2 inches cubed, then that means there are 115 nuggets to a gallon. So . . .

$$660,430 \times 115 = 75,949,450$$

nuggets in a swimming pool.